I LIKE BEING ALONE

by Betty Ren Wright

illustrated by Krystyna Stasiak

Chariot Books
DAVID C. COOK PUBLISHING CO.

I felt grumpy. I wasn't sure why.

"This is great!" said my new friend Jason as he looked at the bunk beds in my room. "You're so lucky."

I pointed to a top bunk. "That's mine. The bottom is Gretchen's. My brothers' room is down the hall. Andrew's crib is in my Mom and Dad's room."

4

We went downstairs. Kurt and Peter raced by. Erik and Gretchen were playing a game at the kitchen table. Andrew pushed a truck down the hall. In the living room, Tim watched TV with his friends.

"You're lucky!" Jason said again. "You always have brothers and sisters to play with."

"It's okay," I said. I was thinking about Jason's house, where there are no brothers and sisters. Jason has a bedroom all his own.

I'd like to be alone sometimes too, I thought. Yes, that was what was making me grumpy. I love my family, but they are always right there. Every minute.

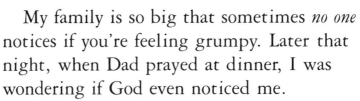

My family is so big that sometimes *no one* notices if you're feeling grumpy. Later that night, when Dad prayed at dinner, I was wondering if God even noticed me.

Aunt Rose could tell, though. "What's the matter, Brenda?" she whispered. "Want to come to my room after dinner?"

Aunt Rose is the only one in the family with her own room. She pays Dad rent for it, and he puts the money in the bank.

11

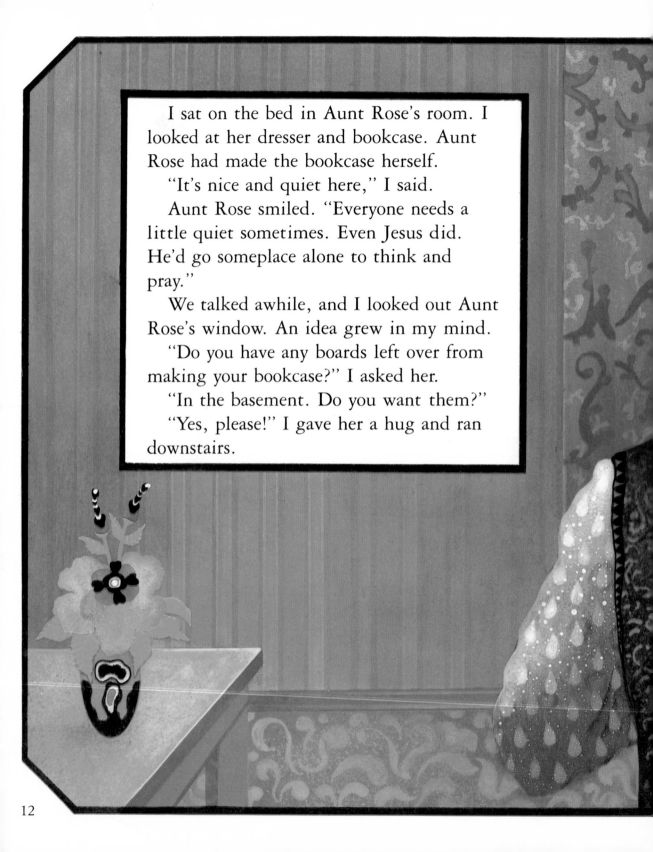

I sat on the bed in Aunt Rose's room. I looked at her dresser and bookcase. Aunt Rose had made the bookcase herself.

"It's nice and quiet here," I said.

Aunt Rose smiled. "Everyone needs a little quiet sometimes. Even Jesus did. He'd go someplace alone to think and pray."

We talked awhile, and I looked out Aunt Rose's window. An idea grew in my mind.

"Do you have any boards left over from making your bookcase?" I asked her.

"In the basement. Do you want them?"

"Yes, please!" I gave her a hug and ran downstairs.

That evening and the next, I worked. I made pencil marks on boards. Aunt Rose helped me saw the boards and nail them together to make a strong platform.

On Saturday I got up early. I carried a ladder to the only tree in our backyard. I pushed the platform into the low branches. Then I climbed up and pulled the platform higher.

Soon I was at the wide, safe place I had seen from Aunt Rose's window. I rested the platform across two thick branches.

This is a nice place, I thought. I wondered if Jesus had ever climbed a tree.

"What are you doing up there, Brenda?" a voice asked from below. It was Dad. He sounded worried.

"I'm sitting in my tree house," I said. "This is my special place, Dad. I made it."

"Hmm. Looks pretty good," he said. "I'll get rope and help you tie it in place."

Everyone came to see my tree house. Aunt Rose brought nails and more boards. She showed me how to make sides around the platform, so I wouldn't slip off.

17

It was a perfect day. I took books and a banana to the tree house. At noon I ate my lunch there. It was strange to eat alone, with only the birds for company.

When I went back to the house, I felt as if I had been very far away. *I like being alone*, I thought, *and I like being with other people too*.

19

That night I asked, "Could I sleep in my tree house tonight, please?"

Mom and Dad looked at each other.

"You'll be lonesome," said Dad.

"I'll miss you," Gretchen said.

"I think it sounds like fun," said Aunt Rose.

"I guess it would be okay," Mom said.

I put on my pajamas, and found a sleeping bag and a flashlight.

"Just come inside if you change your mind," said Dad.

I shook my head. I had my own room at last — well, mine and God's. The biggest room in the world! The sky was the ceiling.

I lay awake a long time. I listened to the crickets, and the sounds of the city all around our house.

I thought about things I might do when I grow up.

I could see the moon through the branches, and I said, "Hi, old moon," right out loud.

I watched the lights go out in our house.

I woke up in the middle of the night. The wind was blowing hard. The tree seemed to bend and sigh. Leaves skittered across my face. The moon was gone, and it was very dark.

I looked out at the blackness. Then I heard a noise. It was something below the tree. Something alive. I could hear its feet rustling through the leaves.

I tried to pray. Or scream. Nothing came out. I just wanted to slide down into the sleeping bag and close my eyes tight.

But I knew I had to find out what was there, or else I'd be too scared to sleep in my tree house again.

I found the flashlight and leaned over the edge of the platform. "Who's there?" I asked in a shaky voice.

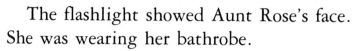

The flashlight showed Aunt Rose's face. She was wearing her bathrobe.

"Are you all right?" she asked. "When the wind started, I thought you might be afraid."

I took a deep breath. "I'm fine, thanks," I called softly. I was so glad I had looked. If I hadn't, I would have been scared all night.

"Sleep well, then," said Aunt Rose. I heard her steps going away.

I lay back in my sleeping bag. The moon peeked out from behind a cloud.

"Tomorrow I'll let the others take turns sitting in my tree house," I whispered to God. "But it will still be my place when I want to be alone."

The answer seemed to come sighing on the wind. *I understand. Your very own place.* And then I fell asleep.